RIGHT HERE WAITING

T.A. MCKAY

COPYRIGHT © T.A. MCKAY, 2017
ALL RIGHTS RESERVED

COVER ART BY FRANCESSCA'S PR & DESIGN
FORMATTING BY: T.A. MCKAY

THIS IS A WORK OF FICTION. NAMES, CHARACTERS, PLACES AND INCIDENTS ARE EITHER THE PRODUCT OF THE AUTHORS IMAGINATION OR USED FACTIOUSLY AND ANY RESEMBLANCE TO ACTUAL PEOPLE, DEAD OR ALIVE, BUSINESS, ESTABLISHMENTS, LOCALES OR EVENTS IS ENTIRELY COINCIDENTAL. ANY REFERENCE TO REAL EVENTS, BUSINESSES OR ORGANIZATIONS IS INTENDED ONLY TO GIVE THE FICTION A SENSE OF REALISM AND AUTHENTICITY.

ALL RIGHT RESERVED. NO PART OF THIS PUBLICATION MAY BE REPRODUCED, STORED IN A RETRIEVAL SYSTEM, OR TRANSMITTED BY ANY MEANS – ELECTRONIC, MECHANICAL, PHOTOGRAPHIC (PHOTOCOPYING), RECORDING OR OTHERWISE – WITHOUT PRIOR PERMISSION IN WRITING FROM THE AUTHOR.

PIRATING AN AUTHOR'S WORK IS A CRIME AND WILL BE TREATED AS SUCH.

DEDICATION

Dedication

This story was originally written to support Worldwide Cancer Research & The Male Cancer Awareness Campaign. So I dedicate this book to all the survivors out there. May you continue to win the fight.

PROLOGUE

Fourteen Months Earlier

Tristen

"Are you really trying to convince me that you meant the garlic bread to look like that? Babe, it's burnt."

I glare at Ray as I try to scrape off the worst of the charcoal. I have never claimed to be a great cook, and to be honest I'm not even a slightly good one. "It's not burnt, it's well fired."

Ray's laughter fills the small kitchen and as much as I'm trying to be angry with him, I smile as I continue to scrape the black top layer off the bread. I'm still smiling when his arms slip around my waist and he kisses my cheek before resting his chin on my shoulder.

"I'm glad I'm not with you for your cooking ability. Thankfully you are really good in bed." When he finishes speaking he digs his fingers into my sides and I drop the knife and bread, crying out as he tickles me. I hate being tickled and he knows it.

I twist in his arms until I'm facing him, throwing my arms around his neck and pulling him close enough to kiss. When I brush my lips over his he stops his assault on my side and grips my arse in his hands, pulling me in closer. I love when he gets like this, it makes me feel secure and wanted. It also makes me horny and I'm sure he will be able to tell that by the hard on that's growing in my jeans.

"Mmm ... I love that you respond so quickly." His words come out on a groan and I know that he's noticed how hard I am.

"I love that you love that I respond so quickly."

"And I love that you love that I love..."

I silence him with a deeper kiss and tighten my arms around his neck. This man right here is my life. He is the reason that I wake up in the morning with a smile on my lips and he's also the reason that I go to bed at night satisfied. I didn't ever imagine I would meet someone like him. I thought I had had my chance at love with my ex Garry and when he cheated on me, I thought that my chance had gone. Garry was my everything. My friend, my lover, my soul mate. Unfortunately he was also that for someone else. I want to be angry with him still but if I was still with him I wouldn't be with the guy that's in my arms right now, and I wouldn't want a life without Ray.

He pulls back slightly until his lips are just brushing over mine. "Are you hungry?"

"No." I should feel ashamed of how breathy my answer sounds but this is his fault. He does something to me when he kisses me and I always find it difficult to catch my breath. I always read stories about people who were in love, about how they would swoon when the object of their affection was near, and I would laugh. I mean how is it even possible to be affected by someone like that? Now I know.

"That's the right answer, beautiful." He takes me by the hand and starts to lead me down the hall towards our bedroom. I follow him closely, trying not to look too eager about what's about to happen, but I know I fail when I see Ray's crooked smile. He really is the sexiest man I've ever seen with his red hair and green eyes. He isn't what I would call my usual type when it came to the men I used to go after, but the night I went to the club and saw him smiling on the opposite side of the dance floor I knew I wanted him

Even after all this time Ray makes my heart race when I see him and I know he is the man I'm going to spend the rest of my life with. I want to get married and grow old with him while surrounded by cats. We need to travel the world and get pictures in every single country before we settle down in our little country cottage with a coal fire and bicker like every other old couple I know. That's my dream and I will get it. I've never been more certain of anything in my life.

I STAND AT ONE END OF THE AISLE AND LOOK TOWARDS THE COFFIN at the other end. *I can't go up there.* If I see Ray lying there then it will make this whole thing real and it can't be real, there's no way he would leave me like this. We had our whole lives planned out and if he's gone I don't know what I'm going to do with the rest of my life. No, this is all some bad dream and I need to wake up.

I watch as Ray's mum approaches the coffin, supported by her best friend, and looks inside. She cries out in anguish as she gets close enough to look inside the casket. I can feel her pain as she looks at the body of her son, the agony clear in the sound that's coming from her. I close my eyes, unable to deal with seeing her grief. I want to go to her and tell her that she shouldn't hurt, that she hasn't lost her only son but the more I hear her heart ripping apart, I feel that this might not be the dream I'm hoping it is. I back away, ready to run from the church, when my back connects with hard body. I mumble an apology and get ready to make my escape. I need to get out of here. I can't deal with this, there's no way I can see him lying in there.

Flashbacks from the night Ray died threaten to take my legs from beneath me. Listening to the police tell me that they were sorry and that there was nothing anyone could have done to save his life was the worst moment of my life. Trying to understand when they explained that Ray had been leaving his office when he ran across the road to make the last bus, but he didn't look before he stepped into the road. Because of the surface water on the road the car had been unable to stop and had crushed him against the side of the bus. He died before he arrived at the hospital and the police had got my contact details from his phone. The memory of them asking me to come with them and identify Ray's body had me going into a panic attack like I had never had before. I started sweating and shaking, and after sitting staring at them for what felt like hours I told them I couldn't do it. I couldn't be the one to confirm that he was dead. Even now, almost a week later, the thought of doing it has me feeling faint.

I'm just about to repeat the panic attack from that night when a pair of arms wrap around my waist. My body freezes and my muscles tense at the touch. I turn quickly, moving away from the person and my breath catches. "August?"

"Hey, buddy."

I rush over to him and throw my arms around him. He returns the gesture, putting his arms back around my waist and holding me close to him. For the first time in days I feel like I can breathe and I melt into his embrace as I let my emotions go.

"I'm so sorry, Tristen. So fucking sorry."

I tighten my hold around his neck and give into the tears I've held back since the accident. I don't know how long we stand there but it's August who pulls back before cupping my face and drying my tears with his thumbs. He looks like he's going to talk but instead he takes my hand and leads me outside into the bright sunshine. The weather has been nice since the night of the accident, the night that took away the most important thing in my life. The rain hadn't been predicted and I've often found myself wondering if it had been sent just to take the love of my life away from me. I know that's dramatic and that the world doesn't work like that but it's the only thing that makes sense to my confused mind.

August pushes me down onto a bench that's just outside the church doors and sits down close to my side whilst holding my hand. I close my eyes and lean my head back against the wall, letting the sun heat the skin on my face.

"I know this is a really stupid question, but how're you doing?"

I don't open my eyes when I answer him. "I will be a lot better once I wake up. I just want to wake up." I feel his hand tighten around mine and I just enjoy the feeling of having someone here for me. No, not just someone, I needed my best friend. August is the only person I would want here with me just now.

"You know that isn't going to happen, mate. You just need to make it through today and say goodbye. I know it's hard but you just need to keep breathing. I'm here to hold you up."

"The last time I saw him he looked so handsome. He was wearing the blue shirt I got him for Christmas and it made his eyes pop. As a person he was just so alive and that's how I want to remember him. I can't see him when he's no longer *him*, I can't see him without the sparkle in his eyes."

I feel August move closer to me and his hands cup my face. I try not to look into his eyes but his hold on my face is strong and he forces me to look up. "You haven't seen him?"

I try to shake my head but his grip limits my movements. It doesn't stop the tears that roll down my cheeks and I see the sympathy in August's eyes. I've held myself together the last few days but having him here is breaking down the walls I've built around my grief. No one gets me the way August does, not even Ray could understand me in the same way. "I can't."

August's thumbs rub over my cheeks, wiping the tears that refuse to stop falling. "You have to, Tristen. If you miss your chance to say goodbye you will regret it. Maybe not today, or tomorrow, but one day you will wake up and the fact that you didn't say goodbye will rip you apart."

I don't want to believe him but I know I'm not thinking straight at the moment, my grief clouding my judgement, so there's a good chance that August is right. As much as I tell myself that seeing Ray is the last thing I want to do, I trust August enough to take his advice. "Okay."

A warm smile crosses August's lips and he leans over to kiss my forehead. He hasn't done that since we were both twelve and Freddie Craig told me he liked girls and not boys. Freddie was my first crush after I realised that I liked boys but he also turned out to be my first heartbreak. August was there for me through the whole thing. The gentle kiss gives me more comfort than I would ever admit to anyone and it makes me notice just how much I've missed August being around. For the first time since Ray died, I feel like I might just survive.

The feeling vanishes quickly when August takes my hand and leads me back into the church. My heart starts to race and it makes my pulse beat loudly in my ears. I know my death grip on his hand must hurt but he doesn't once complain or try to remove himself from my grasp.

At the end of the aisle he allows me to pause for a moment to try and compose myself. His thumb rubs over the back of my hand and I use the movement to focus my laboured breathing. *In and out. In and out.* August doesn't realise it but he has the ability to calm me by just being near and I've always been thankful to have him as my best friend.

With a squeeze of my hand August starts forward again. I don't want to do this but with August by my side I can.

I TIP THE SHOT GLASS AGAIN, DRAINING IT IN ONE BEFORE motioning to the barman for a refill. I know it's not the healthiest way to deal with my grief but I can't think of a better way tonight. I can feel August's stare burning into the side of my head but he doesn't say a word as I down another tequila. Warmth spreads through my body as my thoughts become slightly more blurred. This is what I was looking for, the numbness that only alcohol can bring. Even with my drunken haze and August sitting quietly to my side, I can feel the burning desire inside him to speak. "Out with it." I don't look at him as I speak, instead I focus on the bottle of beer on the bar in front of me.

"I was just wondering what you're going to do now. I don't want to leave you here alone."

I don't want to think about August leaving because I don't know what I will do without him. I haven't seen much of August the last few years, actually now that I think about it, I haven't seen him since I got together with Ray. When the relationship started we kind of drifted apart. We still speak on the phone regularly but it's not the same as seeing each other and spending time together. Now the thought of going back to not seeing August is scaring me. As selfish as it is, with my life going to shit I need my best friend to make me feel better. "I haven't thought that far ahead yet. When do you have to leave?"

"I could only get a few days. Work is crazy right now and I have to get back."

It's the same reason he always gives me for not being able to visit and for the first time, it pisses me off. I know he lives a good few hours drive away, but I'm sure that he could get a day off here and there.

"Yeah, I'm sure that they won't be able to cope without you." The words come out more sarcastic than I'd intended and they are met with silence. I risk a look in August's direction and I wish I hadn't. The pain in his eyes makes me instantly feel like shit.

I've already lost the man I love and I shouldn't be pushing away the only other person in this world I care about. It's not August's fault that I have no fucking idea what to do next. "I'm sorry, I'm taking this out on you and I have no right to. I have no idea what I'm going to do and I'm trying not to think about how fucked up everything is. I can't afford the house anymore because Ray's life insurance didn't cover the mortgage for more than a few months, and when that runs out I'm going to be homeless."

I'm met with silence again and it's starting to grate on me a little. I don't expect August to magically have all the answers but any advice would be better than silence. I tap the bar in front of me to get the barman's attention. I know I'm coming across as a dickhead to him, but in the grand scheme of things it's the least of my worries. I watch as my shot glass is refilled, thinking I should probably thank the guy but still I don't. I pick it up and just as I empty it into my mouth August speaks, causing the tequila to get stuck in my throat.

After a coughing fit that feels like it takes an hour to get under control, I turn to August with tear filled eyes. "What did you say?"

He plays with his beer bottle before finally looking up at me. "I said move in with me."

CHAPTER ONE

Present Day

August

I smile as I hear Tristen walk in through the front door. I'm sitting on the couch waiting on him to get home and the smell of pizza is making my stomach rumble. He texted me earlier to say that he was running late but I'd already ordered the pizza, so I've spent the last twenty minutes watching the clock and trying not to eat the bloody thing by myself.

"I swear I hate that fucking job, I want to burn the place to the ground." Tristen drops his body heavily onto the couch next to mine, causing me to bounce slightly in my seat.

"I wish you would stop with all this gratitude for the job I got you. All this gushing is embarrassing me."

He turns his head where it's lying back on the couch and without even blinking, raises his hand and gives me the finger. I burst out laughing before leaning forward and finally taking a slice of the cooling pizza. I take a huge bite and the flavour explodes on my tongue making me groan. It's not as hot as I would like and the cheese has solidified a little but after a full day at work it still tastes amazing.

I relax back onto the couch with my slice and watch as Tristen grabs one of his own. I can't help but smile when he struggles to remove his piece without all the toppings falling off. He's such a messy eater and ruins more shirts than anyone else I know. He's actually had to start wearing my shirts because he's running low on work shirts of his own and they haven't faired very well either. I would say it annoys me when he ruins mine, but if I'm honest with myself I'm just happy to see him wearing my clothes. There's something very sexy about another guy wearing your stuff and, even though we aren't in a romantic relationship, I like to see him in my clothes.

He moved here with me the day after Ray's funeral, and I thought it would be a temporary thing but he hasn't mentioned leaving. I didn't think he would have remembered my offer to him but he woke bright and early the next morning, even before I woke up, and was packing before I had my first coffee. By lunchtime he had packed up nearly everything he wanted to take with us and had a van delivered to the house so we could load it. By dinnertime we were on the road for the six-hour drive back to mine with everything he owned in the back. I didn't even have my spare room ready for him to move into, it was still full of boxes from when I moved in, but he didn't care, he just slept in my bed for three nights until we were organised. I was tempted to tell him to just stay in my room but I knew it would be a weird thing to offer no matter how much I would have personally liked it.

That was fourteen months ago and I've been living on cloud nine ever since. It took him a few months to start acting like himself again, his grief became almost too much at one point and I was really worried about him. But he worked through it and when he came out the other side he was stronger than I've ever seen him. That's when I got him a job at the computer tech company where I work and he's been there for just under a year now. I actually thought he would be located in my office but he showed a natural ability for numbers so they moved him to the accounting office across town. As much as I would have liked to be able to have lunch with him, I can't complain about it since we get to spend every single night together.

"I can't believe you are gonna be thirty in a few weeks."

My comment makes the slice of pizza freeze on its way to Tristen's mouth and his head turns slowly towards me. He glares and I struggle to hold in my laugh. He's been trying to ignore the fact that he's turning the big three-zero but I refuse to let him. Its maybe not what a good friend would do but he's almost a year older than me so I need to take the piss out off him for it. I mean, he's turning *thirty*. His life is nearly over.

"Shut the fuck up."

I put on my best shocked face and play as innocent as I can. "Such language. I would think you would have a better vocabulary at your advanced age."

"I will shove this pizza up your nose, August."

I bite the inside of my cheek to hold in the laughter. He is far too easy to wind up and I get such pleasure from it. "And the violence, do you think it's the menopause?"

He moves quicker than I would have expected and before I have a chance to move I'm on my back with Tristen straddling my body, his slice of pizza still in his hand. I try to fend him off but I'm laughing so hard that I can't find the strength to push him off me. The second the pizza hits my face I know that there's going to be a lot of cleaning up to do because there's no way he's getting away with this shit. I close my eyes as the tomato sauce starts to smear over my face and reach my hands out blindly, hoping to grab something that will help me win this fight. I manage to get a hold of the front of his shirt and when I do, I hold tight and roll us both until the couch vanishes from below us. We are airborne for a few seconds before we land with a thump, me on top of Tristen, on the floor in between the coffee table and sofa. Tristen grunts at the impact and drops the pizza somewhere on the floor.

I open my eyes and blink several times to get the sauce out of them and look down to make sure I haven't hurt him. He isn't injured, in fact he's still glaring at me and it's all the proof I need to know he's fine. I grab his wrists as he tries to push me off but thanks to my larger size I easily pin his arms to the floor. I drag his hands across the carpet until I can lean my knees on them, leaving my hands free for my payback. "Oh, would you look at that. I do think I have the upper hand now. Hmmm, I wonder how I can repay you for the tomato sauce facial you gave me?"

His glare softens, making him look like he isn't thinking of all the different ways he wants to hurt me. "August, bro, mate. You know I was only messing around. Let's forget all this and watch a movie." He shakes his head as he speaks, causing his thick blonde hair to fall over his forehead. I was always jealous of his hair when we were growing up. My dark seemed so boring next to his lighter, naturally highlighted style, so much so that there was a hair dying accident that resulted in me having orange hair for about a week.

"Let me up, this is silly."

Oh, he would just love it if I let him up and forgot the whole thing. He's always quick to start these things but as soon as he starts to lose he tries to talk his way out of it. When we were younger he was always taller than me and he used that to his advantage. That was until puberty hit, affecting both of us differently. At the age of fourteen Tristen starting to grow and it happened quickly until he hit his full height of five foot eleven. He towered over my small stance and it was eight months of pure hell with Tristen continuously patting me on the head and calling me shorty. Thankfully Karma helped me get my own back and within four months I was towering over his short arse and I couldn't be happier. I also bulked up more than he did, my muscles becoming toned and strong without ever visiting a gym. This is why he relies on surprise attacks. His speed is better than mine but I can usually get the better of him quickly with my strength, and as I stare down at my captive he knows that I'm going to win this one as well.

I turn to see if any of the pizza is within arms reach but we must have knocked the box when we left the sofa because it's over on the other side of the table. I take a second to think about how to exact my revenge as Tristen wriggles in my hold, trying to escape.

"Come on, August. This is stupid. We're grown men and I'm sure a food fight doesn't class as an adult activity."

"Some of us are older than others."

The look he gives me tells me that if I didn't have him pinned he would be attacking me again. "Screw you, August."

I smile at him and I see the moment worry takes over his anger. I think someone needs to learn a lesson here. He really needs to learn that he shouldn't start anything he can't finish.

"Why are you smiling like that? What are you going to do?"

I just keep smiling as I lower my head towards his. He works out quickly what I'm about to do and his struggling increases, almost knocking me from his body. I tighten my legs against his hips and put my hands down on the side of his head just in time to catch myself before I end up lying next to him on the carpet. The move puts my face just above his and I close the last few inches of distance, rubbing my face over his and sharing the tomato facial he just gave me. As sadistic as it sounds, his shriek fills my heart with so much joy that I can't help but laugh at his discomfort.

My laughter continues until he turns his head suddenly and his lips brush over mine. The act is completely innocent but it doesn't stop my stomach from tumbling and my heart racing. I freeze my movements and stare at Tristen whilst trying to keep my face as neutral as possible. I can't let him see how this is making me feel and that means I need to get off him quickly. Just that brief touch of Tristen's lips has my body going crazy and my dick getting hard without permission. I release Tristen's arms and move off him as fast I can, hoping that he won't notice what's going on in my trousers.

I get to my feet and offer Tristen a hand which he takes without hesitation. I pull him up and he stands easily. He's smiling by the time he's fully upright and I grin smugly at the mess I've managed to make of his face.

"One of these days you're not gonna be able to use your ape size to win. I will get the better of you."

"You keep believing that. But this *winner* is going to grab a shower, then we maybe can eat the pizza instead of wearing it." I pat him on the shoulder as I leave the room, using this as the perfect excuse to leave and get myself under control. I walk straight to my ensuite shower and strip off my clothes, stepping under the shower before it even has a chance to warm.

Moments like that keep catching me out and I wish that I didn't react this way with Tristen. I didn't realise that living with him would heighten my already strong attraction. I convinced myself that I knew him as much as I could, but spending this time with him has shown me the kind of man he's actually grown into, and I'm finding him harder to resist than the teenage Tristen I fell in love with. Yeah, falling for your best friend isn't the healthiest thing, but that's the truth of my life.

The minute I met him I knew that I wanted him in my life forever, and even though we were only six-year-old boys, I planned on making that happen.

What I didn't know at the time is that I would fall so madly in love with him that it would actually hurt to see him with someone else. I know Tristen always wondered why I never visited when he moved in with Ray and that's why. Watching him fall head over heels in love with Ray broke my heart and I couldn't force myself to act happy for him. It was easier on the phone to fake my excitement, and after many phone calls I actually got drunk to forget the joy he had found with Ray. I never wanted him to lose Ray the way he did, and I had resigned myself to never telling him how I really feel, but I can't deny that I have loved getting to know this new Tristen.

He's still the fun loving guy that I remember from our childhood, but there's more depth to him now. He's driven at work and already dedicated to the career he has only just recently discovered. I didn't know that I found ambition so sexy but on Tristen it is. He lights up when he talks about his day and you can see his love for it even when he's complaining about it.

Then there is his compassion, he's kind and treats everyone with respect and care. *God he really is the perfect man.* He's always been the sexiest man I've known, even in high school when I fell for him, but he's grown into a man that no one will ever be able to compare to. This makes it really difficult when I think about the fact that he will probably never see me as anything other than his best friend. I keep telling myself that I need to come clean and explain to him how I felt. Tell him that I'm in love with him and I think I always have been but I'm just not brave enough. I don't want to change or even potentially ruin our relationship and that confession would do just that.

I grab the shampoo and concentrate on washing the sauce out of my hair. I need to make a decision about Tristen and stick to it. I need to grow a pair, and consequences be damned, tell him how I feel, or I need to move on and try to find someone I could be happy with. This limbo is driving me insane and I don't think I can live like this for much longer. Now if I could just decide what the fuck I'm going to do that would be great.

I'm lying in my bed watching a movie on Netflix when I hear a quiet knock on the door. "Come in."

Tristen pokes his head around the edge of my door, smiling as he speaks. "You want some company?"

I mute the TV and sit up a bit, leaning back against my headboard. "Always."

As soon as he enters the room I wish I'd pretended I was asleep. Tristen closes the door behind him and makes his way to what I class as his side of the bed. He's always taken the left hand side whenever we've shared so I've always automatically slept on the right, even when he isn't in bed with me. I try not to stare at him as he moves but it's really bloody hard not to when he is only wearing a pair of jogging bottoms. His hair is still damp from the shower he must have just had and his chest is shiny making me wonder if he just applied lotion. I want to run my hands all over his body to see how soft his skin really is.

Fuck me, I need to stop thinking of him like that. Just remember, *best friend*. I distract myself by taking a drink from the bottle of water next to my bed. This isn't the first time that Tristen has walked about half naked, and if I didn't know better I would say he was trying to kill me by making me crave his sexy body more.

He slips in below the sheet and I can smell his aftershave instantly. I nearly sprint from my room to escape the temptation but instead I turn off the bedside light, leaving us with only the movie illuminating the room. It might make things a little more intimate but in my head it provides a layer of darkness to cover anything that might ... arise.

"What are you watching?"

It takes me a moment to remember because the blood in my body is rushing away from my brain but when I do I cringe because he's going to laugh at me. "Beastly."

I can feel his stare but I refuse to look at him. He can just as easily talk shit about me if I don't make eye contact. "I might be getting close to menopause but you are letting your teenage girl hormones show. Beastly isn't a film a man should be watching."

"Like you're The Proposal DVD hasn't been played so often that it needs replacing." I turn to look at him, our faces closer than should be comfortable.

"Erm, hello? Ryan Reynolds."

Okay he's got me there, but there is one thing he's forgetting about what I'm watching. "Erm, hello? Alex Pettyfer."

"Oh, I forgot about him. Turn the volume up and let me watch." He wiggles his eyebrows before turning to look at the TV and I do as he instructs.

I look at the screen myself but my mind is far away. My entire awareness is on the man lying next to me. The deep breaths that he takes as he relaxes, the way he rubs his foot against the sheet without noticing, and I don't even have to look at him to know he's chewing his bottom lip. He does it automatically when he's watching a movie. I've spent most of my life wanting to bite that lip for him. I've seen a lot of men do the same thing but it hasn't done anything for me. Usually I think that they need to stop because they look stupid, but not Tristen. No, his glistening lips and slight teeth marks make my dick hard every single time.

"Do you want me to leave?"

I'm pulled out of my thoughts by his sudden question and it takes me a minute to catch up. "No, you can watch the end of the movie."

He looks away from me and it worries me a little. Tristen never looks nervous around me and I start to wonder why he is now. "I didn't mean tonight. I mean do you want me to move out?"

Words are stuck in my throat, not knowing what to say. *He wants to leave? What did I do?*

CHAPTER TWO

Tristen

I don't know why I feel so nervous bringing this up. It should be a simple question to which he will give me his honest answer. I've wanted to ask him this for a few months but I've never found the courage to do it. I mean what do I do if he says yes? As much as I would love to ignore the whole conversation I know I can't, and broaching the subject first seemed less painful than him telling me to leave.

He hasn't even hinted that he wants me to go, but I know he's probably getting bored having me around. I haven't seen him go out once since I moved in and I don't want him to start resenting me for his lack of social life.

"Why the fuck do you think I want you to leave?" He sounds angry and it makes me look away from him, even though he can't see me clearly in the darkened room.

"I don't know really, I'm just worried that I might be cramping your style. I don't want you to feel like you have to look after me, you have your own life to live."

August sits up and reaches out to turn on the lamp that's on his side of the bed. I match his position, crossing my legs and leaning my elbows on my knees. "Have I ever made you feel that I don't want you here? That you're somehow ruining things for me?"

I lower my head because I don't want to look at him. I've never felt awkward with August but I'm getting much more out of this arrangement than he is, and admitting that is showing how pathetic I actually am. He brought me here when my life was collapsing around me and gave me everything I needed: support, a home and eventually a job. He's been here for me pretty much twenty-four hours a day since Ray died and I haven't given him anything in return. "No, but this situation can't be great for you. You haven't been on a single date since I came along and I can't help but feel that it's my fault. You've put your life on hold and I'm feeling guilty as hell about it."

August's laughter makes me look up because it's a sudden departure from the anger and it's not the response I was expecting. "What sort of life do you think I had before you moved here? I can assure you that I wasn't exactly a hit with the guys. No secret love affair in my past I'm afraid, just me being boring and alone. So really, you being here is actually a good thing, you keep me company." He lies down on his side of the bed and when he turns the light off I follow suit

"I don't believe you by the way." Staring into the darkness I feel him moving on the bed beside me and when he speaks he sounds a lot closer than he was before.

"About what?"

"You not being a hit with guys. There's no way you haven't had men lining up around the corner." I know I'm probably biased, but I think August is one of the most amazing men I've ever met. Even if you don't fall in love with his kindness and generosity, you will fall for how sexy he is. He has that whole tall, dark and handsome thing working for him. Since his growth spurt in high school, no one has been able to hold a candle to him in the looks department. I don't think he truly knows how attractive he is, always playing down his looks when you give him a compliment. He seems to think that I only tell him how attractive he is to be nice, but little does he know how many times I jerked off while picturing him in his PE kit.

"I hate to burst your bubble but I'm not interested in dating. There hasn't been anyone that caught my attention like … they need to."

The hesitation at the end of his sentence peaks my interest. It sounded like he was going to say a name but changed his mind. Is August hiding something from me? "Like ... they need to? That little stutter tells me there's a story that I need to hear. Is there someone important out there, August?" I flip onto my stomach and lay my head onto my arms, getting comfortable for the story but the only thing I'm met with is silence. "Come on, spill it."

He sighs before speaking and I smile as I think about all the juicy details I'm about to get. August has never been one to share about his love life without me pushing and it's been a long time since I turned the spotlight on him. "There was just someone I liked but it was never going to happen. Timing was just always wrong so I never went for it. Sometimes you just have to know when it's time to move on, and eventually I had to understand that I was just not his type."

"Are you crazy, August? Why would you give up on someone without even finding out how they felt?"

"I just didn't see the point in ruining a friendship. Can we drop this? It didn't happen and I'll get over it. Let's talk about something more interesting ... like your birthday."

I don't want to drop the subject. I want to know why August never went after this guy. He has always been the same, it's like there's always something holding him back from pursuing happiness. I was hoping that once I had found Ray that he would see how great it was to have someone in your life but I think it made him retreat even further into himself. In all of the years that I've known August he has never had a relationship that progressed past a couple of dates and I hate to see him alone because he really is the most amazing person I know.

"Do we really need to talk about me getting older? I would much rather continue the conversation about you liking this man."

"Nope, not happening. What do you want to do to celebrate?"

I turn and face the ceiling, biting my lips as I think about my last birthday. It was a few months after Ray had died and I spent the whole day sitting on the couch refusing to acknowledge it. I can't believe that it was a whole year ago. My grief has been a lot easier to live with in the last six months or so and it's all because of August. He made sure that I understood that it was okay to get on with my life because Ray wouldn't want me to sit in and fade away from the world. I think I knew it myself but hearing him tell me it made all the difference. Now just over a year later I feel that I've found myself again, and even though I'm not the same person anymore, I'm finding happiness in my new life. "I really don't know. I suppose I should do something, right?"

"Yes you need to do something. You're gonna be thirty, Tristen. It's an important birthday and I don't want to let it pass without celebrating in style, you've missed out on enough recently."

Again he's right. I've put my life on hold for a long time now and I need to start living again. I started to heal when I made the decision to celebrate the time I had with Ray instead of mourning him, but I haven't really done that yet. I need to get out there, meet new friends and just enjoy myself. I love spending time with August and we have developed a routine that we are both comfortable with, and I think that's become a problem. I've become dependent on him and that's not fair to either of us. No, I need to stand on my own two feet and give him a chance to live his own life. I think my birthday is the perfect opportunity for that. "What do you suggest?"

"How about a night out? We could invite some people from work and head to Olympus to get our dance on."

"I think that sounds like a bloody fantastic idea." And I'm not just trying to keep August happy, it really does sound great. I haven't had a night out in longer than I can remember, even when Ray was alive. When we met we quickly got into the habit of staying in when we spent our nights together. Neither of us were big party animals so there was never any great need to go out and dance the night away. We preferred to spend our time watching movies or cooking. We always joked that we were getting old before our time, but we were just happy being together.

"*Really?* I was sure you'd say no, but I'm glad that you didn't. I will organise it all so you don't need to do a thing."

"Just tell me when to look pretty and I'll make sure that I get my hair done."

His laughter makes me smile like it always does. There's something satisfying about making August happy and as I fall asleep I think about what else I can do to make that smile a more permanent feature on his face.

"So Mikey and Craig are definitely coming. Ryan is a yes if he can get someone to take his daughter for the night, and well, you know that Amy and Chele are always up for a night out."

We are sitting at the dining table eating after another long day at work. This is our normal routine and it's comforting in its predictability. I skewer a few pieces of pasta onto my fork as I listen to August tell me about what he's planned already, stopping the forkful halfway to my mouth so I can ask a question. "What about Robert and Michael?"

"Oh yeah, they're coming too. It should be a good night. I said we would meet them at Olympus at ten." August looks really excited with the night he has planned for me, and with the people that he's invited he should be. I was a little worried about who he would invite since we are in different offices now, but he has a good mixture from both and I really like the people who are coming. I'm glad that it won't be a huge crowd of people because I'm not sure I would be able to cope with that for my first time out. It's more than enough for me to have a good night but not too many to make me feel awkward.

"They're okay with going out to a gay club?" I've never hidden my sexuality from anyone and when I moved here people obviously knew that I had lost my boyfriend, but I know that a lot of straight men aren't comfortable going to a gay club.

"Yeah they're fine with it. It's your birthday so they are willing to go anywhere you want. I'm not saying that the guys won't take a few minutes to settle but they'll get over it. I'm not exactly going to take you somewhere you won't have fun."

"I haven't been out in over a year, I'm pretty sure that I'll have fun no matter where we go. But I suppose it will make it easier for you to pick someone up if we know the men there like dick." I expect to hear laughter but I get nothing from him. Yet again talking to August about him finding someone or going out on a date shuts down the conversation. I don't know why he does it and the only reasons I can think about for him avoiding the subject makes my stomach hurt. I worry that he has either lost a relationship because he's looking after my needs, or maybe he's secretly seeing someone and doesn't want to tell me incase my feelings get hurt. I'm just about to ask him about it when he speaks.

"Are you going to be looking for someone?"

That's a really good question, and it's one I haven't actually thought about. If he had asked me a few months ago I would have flat out told him no, that the last thing I was thinking about was dating anyone, but now I don't know. Maybe that's what I should be doing? How long do I grieve before I'm meant to move on? "I don't think so."

"That's not a definite no. Have you thought about meeting anyone?"

"Truthfully? No. Going out and hooking up with someone isn't something that's even entered my head. I don't how to explain it. I've not felt the need to find someone but it's not really due to my grief anymore. It feels more like I just want more time. Maybe I just need to be alone for a while so I can work out what I need." Now that I've said the words out loud it makes a lot of sense. I was with Ray for a few years, and I honestly thought I would be with him for the rest of my life. Now things need to change and I don't think I should rush into making any big decisions.

August takes a drink from his glass and nods his head at me. "I suppose that makes sense. Just do me a favour, let me know when you're ready to start dating again."

It's a strange request but I suppose after everything he's done for me it isn't exactly too much to ask. It is his house after all and if I'm going to be bringing men home at some point I really should give him the heads up. "You'll be the first on my list, but I don't think you will have to worry about that any time soon. Talking about dating, if you ever need me to make myself scarce for the evening while you entertain, I will be more than happy to find something to do. I don't want you turning into a monk just because I live here." This gets a laugh from August and I smile around a mouthful of pasta.

"I don't think you will have to worry about that. I've gone so long without sex I think my virginity has grown back."

I choke on my mouthful of food and have to grab my napkin to try and stop it from spraying all over the table. When I finally stop choking I throw my napkin at August. "Don't say shit like that when I'm eating. Are you trying to kill me?"

"What? It's the truth. I think the last time I was with a guy I was still wearing Captain America underwear."

"Wasn't that just last week?"

I don't duck quick enough and end up wearing a handful of pasta salad. I look down at myself and watch as a large piece of pasta slides down the front of my shirt before joining the pile that's formed on my lap. It's only been a few days since our pizza fight and now I'm covered in more bloody food. "Seriously? Will we ever be able to go a whole week without one of us being covered in food?"

"I can't see it if I'm being honest."

This has apparently become our thing. The first time it started was three months after I moved in. I had just received some of Ray's belongings from his mum and I was feeling a little sensitive. August had brought home Chinese food but my mood had been shitty. I had picked a fight the whole way through the meal, choosing to take my anger out on him. We were about half way through the dinner when he threw the first spoonful of fried rice. After the shock wore off the whole thing quickly descended into a messy chaos of flying food. By the time we were finished we were sitting opposite each other on the kitchen floor, our backs against the units, and the floor littered with food. It took us nearly two hours to clean it afterwards, but I hadn't felt so free in a long time.

It was maybe our first food fight but it wasn't the last. Sometimes I can't believe the mess we make when it happens, we've even had to repaint the living room because of the stains left by barbeque sauce, but it doesn't stop us from doing it over and over again. As I sit here now, wearing August's dinner, I know there's a good chance that we're going to be repainting again.

CHAPTER THREE

August

"Are you nearly ready? We're going to be late." I forgot how long it takes Tristen to get ready. In college we were always at least an hour late to everything and it was always because Tristen could never decide what to wear. I thought he might have outgrown it but apparently I was wrong.

"Don't rush me."

Nope, nothing has changed. I knock on his bedroom door and enter when I hear him shout. He's standing in the middle of his room, surrounded by what looks like every single piece of clothing he owns, and is staring in his mirror with a disgusted look on his face.

"I look like an idiot."

I'm not sure what Tristen is seeing in the mirror but it's obviously very different from what I can see. He's wearing tight black jeans that look like they are moulded to his arse and a fitted red shirt that shows off his slim waist. His blonde hair is styled to the side, letting the length almost fall over one eyebrow. He is fucking beautiful without even trying and I know that I'm going to spend most of the night trying not to get hard. He makes me look like nothing when standing next to him, but after being his friend for so long I'm used to blending into the background. "Um, what part looks stupid?"

"The whole thing. Not to sound dramatic or anything, but I'm too old to wear my old clothes."

I roll my eyes as I walk up behind him. I want to tell him how sexy he looks and that he's making my dick twitch in my own jeans because he looks so fucking hot, but I can't so I try to convince him with logic. "Too old? Come on man. You're wearing a shirt and some jeans, I'm pretty sure that's a classic combination no matter the age. You're overthinking this. You've told me you aren't going out looking for a man so as long as you're comfortable let's go."

He huffs but runs his hands through his hair before turning to face me. The move causes his hair to stick up in the most adorable way and I know that a lot of men would pay a fortune for the same look. "Fine, let's get out of here before I change my mind and order a pizza.

I laugh at his empty threat but not wanting to take any chances, I leave the room and head towards the front door. I grab my leather jacket and make sure I have my wallet and keys. "Right, let's do this."

We both leave the house and head towards the town centre which is only a ten-minute walk. I want to make tonight amazing for Tristen. Not only because its his birthday, but because I want to show him it's okay to move on. My priority tonight is to make sure that he wants to do it again soon.

I STARE AT THE ATTRACTIVE BLONDE WHO'S GETTING CLOSER TO THE spot where Tristen and I are dancing. I noticed him staring when we walked onto the dance floor and he's been getting progressively closer with each song. He only has eyes for Tristen and I want to take Tristen by the hand and drag him away. I'm trying to be relaxed about the attention he's getting but it's proving difficult to take it all in my stride.

I grab Tristen by the hand and spin him towards me, faking a twirl so I can put my body between him and blonde guy. Tristen laughs before grabbing my waist and pulling me towards him, our hips colliding as he closes his eyes and lets the music take over. I groan at the move, thankful that it won't be heard over the loud music. Maybe dancing with Tristen isn't such a great idea because feeling him pressed against me is just how I remember it from our college days and it feels amazing. Even though he's smaller than me, he fits perfectly and against my better judgement I let my alcohol infused brain take over and grind my groin into him. I can feel myself harden as his stomach rubs against my dick but I don't let it stop me. I run my hands around his waist, letting them linger just above his arse. I want nothing more than to lower them and feel his perfect cheeks fill my palms.

I'm just about to give in to the very bad idea when Mr blonde comes over and leans in to speak into Tristen's ear. I can't hear what's being said, but Tristen moves away from me with a smile appearing on his lips as he turns to speak to the guy. My heart starts racing in my chest as I watch them talk to each other in the middle of the busy dance floor, and even though dancers surround us, I can only see the two men in front of me.

Tristen turns to look at me before he smiles and winks as he starts to walk away with the guy in the direction of the bar.

I didn't think it was possible but I actually feel the moment my heart shatters in my chest. I went through this when Tristen met Ray and I'm not sure I can go through it again. I don't think I can watch this again. I can't watch him fall in love with a man that isn't me. Fuck, would you listen to me. He has gone to the bar with someone he met on a dance floor and I have him falling in love and getting married. I need to stop drinking because it's making me crazy.

Tristen

I stare intently at the guy who approached me on the dance floor. His name is Will and when he first spoke to me my nerves almost had me running away. He's really attractive and instinct told me I shouldn't waste my time talking with him. I've been out of the game for so long that I didn't want to waste such an attractive guys time, especially when he could probably get any other man in here if he wanted. The only thing that gave me confidence to accept his offer of a drink was having August here. I know that if anything were to go wrong he would be close by to rescue me.

The first thing that caught my attention when I turned and saw Will were his eyes. They're dark green or at least that's what they look like under the flashing lights, but it wasn't their colour that stood out, it was the sparkle in them. It made him look like he was hiding a naughty secret and I instantly wanted to know what it was. His almost white blonde hair stood out just as much as his eyes, and the combined effect actually makes him look really young. He assured me that he wasn't as young as he looked and now I'm sitting at a table in the back corner with him having a great time.

I'd enjoyed dancing with August, it's always easy with him and I wasn't sure if I wanted to leave him to chat with Will. I can just let go with August knowing that he won't judge me no matter how bad my dancing is. When he was holding me close to him I felt relaxed and safe. It felt like when we used to go out in college, both of us drunk and dancing provocatively together to get a guys attention. I could always count on August to make me look good out on the dance floor, and going by the fact that Will told me he couldn't stop watching me move, I take it that it still works. As much fun as I was having with August, I'm glad I took the chance to talk to Will.

"I haven't seen you out here before, have you just moved to the area?"

I take a drink from my bottle of beer to buy myself a little time before I answer. I don't really want to get into why he hasn't seen me before but I also don't want to lie to him. I know that I probably won't see Will again after tonight but on the off chance that I do, I give him half of the truth. "I've been here about a year, but it's the first time I've come out. I haven't been in the best place since moving here but I'm having a great time tonight."

Will looks like he wants to ask something else but he doesn't and I'm grateful to him. "Well I'm glad that you decided to come out tonight. I wasn't sure if you would talk to me when I saw you dancing with that guy. You seemed really intimate but I thought I would chance talking to you. Is he your boyfriend?"

I choke on a mouthful of beer, confused by the question. Why would he think that I was in a relationship with August? I know I was dancing with him but there is no way that we looked intimate. "I'm not with August. I was dancing with him but he's just my best friend."

Will looks confused, his forehead scrunching up in a kinda cute way. "Are you sure? You move together like you know each other inside and out."

He's right about that. August really does know me better than anyone else but that's what best friends are. "I'm pretty sure he's not my boyfriend, if he is I missed the memo. He's my best friend and we've known each other since we were kids."

"My mistake. So, what do you like to do in your spare time?"

I forgot about all this small talk stuff and I bite my lip to stop myself from laughing. I always hated this part of pretending to get to know someone before moving on to the more exciting stuff. I'm thinking that Will might want to accelerate the normal time line when I see him staring at my lips intently.

My heart starts racing again when I think about what might happen tonight with Will and how far he might want to take it. Will he be happy with just kissing, and if he is, am I? Can I kiss someone that isn't Ray? I know that I told August that I wasn't ready to move on but sitting here with Will, I'm starting to wonder if I am. He's really fucking cute with his boyish looks and a body that any fitness model would be happy with, and I think any man in here tonight would be happy to get his attention. I've got it though and now that the opportunity has presented itself, I think I'm more than happy to go with the flow and see where the night takes me.

I should have taken my own advice and stopped drinking when Tristen started to talk to Blondie. I should have swapped the alcohol for water but instead I started on spirits and let my anger and pain start to fester inside.

The night had started so well; it was just the two of us having fun.

Despite all of our friends being here with us it felt like it was just him and me, especially when we moved to the dance floor. Now I'm sitting on my own at our table, seething with anger as I see the blonde Adonis make his move on *my* man. I don't know if I'm angrier at how attractive the guy is and how happy Tristen looks with the attention he's getting, or the fact that I can't go over there and tell the world that Tristen is mine. And I can't tell Tristen I want and love him or that I want him to leave the guy and come back to spend time with me. I can't tell him I want to be with him for the rest of my life.

I grab my drink from the table and finish it, wincing at the burn as the liquid slips down my throat. When did life get so fucking hard? I thought I was able to suppress my feelings for Tristen and keep them hidden so I could keep being his friend. Now seeing him moving on after his loss makes me realise I don't know if I can be his friend. He'd said that he wasn't ready to be with anyone else and if he was, he would tell me? I believed what he said and I was using the time to build up the courage to finally tell him how I felt no matter what would happen afterwards. Now he's moved on without giving me a chance to be what he needed. I could have been the guy that gave him everything, who loved him no matter what, but now he's gone and met someone else whilst I was watching. No, I can't do this again. I *refuse* to do this again. I don't think anyone would blame me for not sitting by whilst my heart got broken again.

My breath gets stuck in my throat as I see the guy lean in and brush his lips over Tristen's ear, lingering far longer than needed. When Tristen doesn't back away I've decided I've seen enough. I need to get out of here before I do something stupid like going over there and ripping Blondie away from Tristen.

I stand and grab my jacket from the back of my chair, putting it on as I start to walk to the exit. I should just leave but despite my anger I can't go without letting Tristen know, he might worry about me and I don't want that. I approach them slowly, my nails digging into my palm as I watch them together. The last thing I needed to see as I reached the table was Tristen's hand resting on Blondie's thigh, far too high up to just be friendly.

"I'm leaving." I don't hang around to see if he hears me or not. I told him I was leaving so my conscience is now clear.

I walk out of the nightclub and head down the street towards home. All I want to focus on now is going to bed and nothing more. Any decisions about Tristen can wait until the morning when my head is less foggy, but the way I'm feeling just now, as much as I hated the idea of him leaving, it might actually be the best thing for us. Maybe a little distance would put all this into perspective for me and help me get control over my feelings again.

Just as I turn the corner at the end of the street I'm grabbed by the arm and spun in place, turning me to face the opposite direction. I pull my free arm back, ready to punch my attacker but pause when I see Tristen standing in front of me with a shocked look on his face. For the first time tonight I'm actually glad I've had a drink because it's slowed my reflexes and stopped me from striking out as quickly as I normally would. If I had I'm pretty sure Tristen would be lying on the pavement by now.

"Why did you leave?"

The sound of his voice has my anger showing itself again. I know I'm being unfair to him, he has no idea that I have feelings for him and so doesn't realise that he's hurting me right now, but I just can't seem to let the thought make me relax. "Where did you leave your boyfriend?"

Tristen's forehead screws up and he just stares at me. "What are you talking about? Is this about Will?"

Learning his name doesn't make me feel any better about the situation and I turn to walk away. I only make it a few steps when I'm grabbed again. This time it isn't such a surprise so I pull out of his grasp.

"August, would you just stop?"

I keep walking, letting my hurt and pain fuel me, my pace increasing. I hear Tristen behind me but I don't slow down.

"August, what the fuck is wrong with you?"

I stop instantly, spinning in place until I'm looking straight at Tristen. I should take a minute to think about my overreaction to this, especially since I can see the look of hurt and confusion on Tristen's face, but my emotions just won't let me calm down. "What's wrong with me? You have no fucking idea do you? I swear you act like I need to spell it out for you."

"Fine, spell it out because I don't know what's happening right now."

I should just walk away. I should put distance between us but my brain has lost the little voice that makes sense, leaving me unsupervised with the impulsive part. I storm over to where Tristen stands, stopping when I'm close enough to feel his stuttered breath on my lips. His eyes are wide and his lips parted as I stare at them. I've wanted to do this my entire life and this might be the only chance I ever get to actually do it.

This is my moment. This is my dream. This is everything.

I stop thinking and let my body take over as I lean in and claim Tristen's lips.

CHAPTER FOUR

Tristen

I stand in shock and watch as August storms away from me. *What the hell was that?* My fingers drift upwards and brush over my still tingling lips.

August kissed me, he really fucking kissed me. I would be more shocked about it happening if the fact that I enjoyed it more than I should wasn't messing with my head so much. Oh my god, August *kissed* me. I step backwards until my back hits the wall behind me. I thought tonight might change everything, I just didn't imagine it would be in this way.

At the nightclub I was having fun getting to know Will and as the minutes passed we were becoming more comfortable in each other's company and we started to get closer. Will's lips brushed around my ear as he spoke and the warmth of his breath made my dick wake up quickly. It isn't the first time that I've found interest in someone I've met, but it is the first time I thought I might actually do something about it. I'm pretty sure that's where the night was going, especially when Will's finger brushed over my hard on. I gasped at the intimate connection on my neglected dick.

I was fully on board with the whole thing, or at least I was right up until the moment August appeared and told me he was leaving. The minute he said that my attention was fully on him. I couldn't understand why he was leaving. Was he annoyed that I had left him to talk to Will? Wasn't it August who told me that I should go out and try to meet someone? Okay, he hadn't actually said exactly that, but he had asked if I was thinking of moving on. I hadn't lied to him, because at the time I wasn't interested in hooking up with anyone. Even when we arrived at the club I was happy just to spend time with my friends, but then Will spoke to me and I decided that maybe he was a good place to start with the living again thing.

Now when I think about moving on it isn't Will's face that I see. No, now all I can picture is August and that shocks the shit out of me. I've never thought of August as anything other than my best friend but now as my lips tingle from his kiss, I wonder if there's something else I'm feeling.

Could I possibly like August as more than just a friend?

I think back over the last few months, at all the time we've spent together and I can honestly say that he's the only reason I made it through the past year. He's been so patient and caring, letting me deal with everything at my own pace, and never being pushy about anything. He has made everything about me for as long as I can remember and if he hadn't kissed me tonight I never would have realised that he had feelings for me at all. He's never given any clue that he saw me as anything else other than his best friend, or has he? Have I just been blind to everything and so caught up in my own bullshit that I didn't pay enough attention to August. If that's true then it shows not only am I oblivious to anything that isn't to do with me but it also means I'm a really shit friend. Is it possible that I am so stuck in my own drama that I've missed things that are going on right under my nose?

I push away from the wall and head in the same direction as August had vanished minutes earlier. I don't know what I will say to him when I get home, how to even start a conversation about what just happened? I want to go straight to bed and give myself a chance to think about what I'm feeling. That's the biggest problem with the whole situation, I don't know what I want to say because I don't know what I'm feeling. Half an hour ago I would have been able to tell anyone what my relationship with August was, but in the space of thirty short minutes everything I thought I knew has changed.

I reach the front of our house too quickly and as I push the door open I'm met with complete darkness. I slip inside and take my jacket off, hanging it on one of the pegs on the wall. I move as quietly as I can, listening to see if I can hear August moving about but I'm met with only silence. Common sense says I should go to bed and sleep on this, let the dust settle a bit but I can't do that. The memory of his kiss is just too fresh and confusing in my mind, and I need to talk to him about it now. I need to find out why he did it and where we go from here.

I head down the hall towards August's room. The silence would make me think I was home alone, but since I found the front door unlocked I know that he must be here. It's not only the unlocked door that lets me know he's here though, I swear I can feel him. It's possibly just my imagination but I can actually feel him. There is an air of tension in the air as I walk through the house towards August. I knock on his bedroom door but there's no answer. Again my common sense tells me to leave him alone but I don't listen and I grab the door handle before pushing the door open. His bedside light is on but his room is empty. I can see the light from the ensuite shining through the open door so I head in that direction. Hearing the water running makes it real that he's in there and I feel my stomach churn with nerves. I take a deep breath and walk through the open door.

August is standing at the sink with his hands resting on the edge and his head dropped forward. I can't see his face and I wish I could, I want to be able to gauge his mood but I am going to have to play it by ear. I take another quiet step into the room and even though he keeps his head down, his body tenses so I know that he's realised I'm here. I lean back against the door and cross my arms over my chest. I don't know what to say so I just stand there in silence, watching him as he raises his head and looks at me in the mirror. I try to read his emotions again but his face has remained blank. I've never seen August so closed off and I'm hoping that this situation isn't going to ruin what we have.

"How long?" I don't know why that's the first question that comes to mind, especially when I should be asking why he kissed me and what's going on.

He turns the water off and grabs a towel to dry his face. When he's done he throws it into the hamper beside the shower and turns his eyes back to me, still in the mirror and not turning around. He shrugs at me but doesn't speak.

"You've got to give me something here, August."

He finally turns to face me, leaning back against the sink and crossing his arms over his chest, mimicking my stance. "I don't know what to tell you."

"How about the truth?" I keep my voice level when I want to do nothing more than to shake him by the shoulders. He's being purposely evasive and where I would normally find it pretty funny, it's not going to fly tonight.

"Nah, I don't think that's the best way to go. How about we go to sleep and in the morning we look for somewhere else for you to live?"

My heart starts racing as he speaks. *He wants me to move out?* The other night when I offered I was hoping beyond hope that he would tell me I was being stupid, because even though I made the offer I didn't want to do it. Living with August has been the best year of my life and the thought of moving out makes my heart hurt in my chest. I straighten and step towards August. "Move out? Why?"

When he spoke before he looked confident in his statement but now I can see that flicker of uncertainty. If it had been anyone else I probably wouldn't have seen it, but I know August, or at least I thought I did. "I think it's for the best. I just can't do this anymore."

I take another step towards him and nerves hit me again but this time it's because I'm closer to him. I feel an awareness of August that I've never noticed before. Being around him has never been a big deal to me, we mess around and usually end up lying all over each other, but apparently the kiss has changed something. "I don't want to leave." My voice sounds deeper than normal, full of lust, and it surprises me as much as it does August.

His eyes widen when he hears me and his breathing start to quicken as he drops his arms to his side and grasps the sink edge behind him. "Tristen."

That single word, the way that he breathes my name, has a new reaction flooding my body. Pure hot need has my dick hardening to the point of pain. August is turning me on more just now than I think anyone else has, and that includes Ray. It should feel wrong but all I can feel is all the ways it feels natural, like this was always meant to happen.

I throw caution to the wind and take another step. The full length of my body rubs against August and I tilt my head up so I can watch his reaction. If he looks uncomfortable at any point then I'll back off but when I feel his own erection press against my stomach I know he's feeling the same as I am.

"Fuck, Tristen."

I tilt my hips, knowing that our height difference won't have our cocks rubbing together but the friction from his thigh has fireworks exploding through me. *How did this happen?* When did the feel of August, his touch and voice, create such a reaction in me? Did the kiss awaken something inside me that was always there, lying dormant and just waiting for a chance to show itself? "Why did you kiss me?"

"Because I needed to. I didn't think I would have gotten through the night if I hadn't."

"Do you want to do it again?" I find myself praying that he says yes. I have taken my actions beyond what a friend should do and if he doesn't want this I'm not sure how I'll cope. August has been my best friend for nearly twenty-two years but now I want something very different from him. One simple action has me wanting to know what it feels like to be with August. It's crazy, it's like someone has flipped a switch inside me and now I want my best friend in my bed. I can't explain it. All I know is that an hour ago my life seemed simple and now, well now I want to pin August against the wall and kiss him until he doesn't want anyone else ever again.

"I want to kiss you more than anything. I've wanted to kiss you since I was fourteen and you got that haircut you hated, but I thought it made you the most beautiful person I knew."

My stomach flips at his admission. When I asked him earlier how long he had liked me he never answered but now I know that he's been hiding his feelings for almost half his life. How must that feel, watching me be with other people? I couldn't even imagine going through that. I want to ask him so many things and find out why he's hidden it all these years, but instead I lean forward and kiss him. I have to rise onto my toes a little to reach him properly and when my lips fully connect with his the tingling from earlier starts again, only this time it feels like an explosion. I gasp into his mouth and it allows him to stroke his tongue over mine. This is it, this is the turning point in my life when everything changes but finally makes sense.

As dramatic as my thoughts sound I know that I truly believe them. I have spent most of my life talking to August, telling him everything and letting him into every part of my life. Every part except this one and all I can think is *why didn't I kiss August before tonight?*

August's arms wrap around my waist and I swear I swoon against him like some character from an old love story. I didn't think it was possible to feel this good just from kissing someone. It's like all the stars have aligned in this one moment and light is shining down on us from above. I would laugh at my inner monologue sounding like some love sick teenager but August chooses that moment to grab my arse and pull me as close to him as possible, making all coherent thought vanish from my head.

I'm lost in the feel of August's tongue when he pulls away, leaving me groaning with frustration. I open my eyes, needing to blink a few times to focus again. When my vision rights itself I see August staring at me, his eyes sparkling as he looks at me.

"I have wanted to do that for so long. I don't know what this means to you, but I want you to know that it isn't the alcohol that's making me do this. I needed to know what it was like to kiss you, and even if you don't want anything more with me I will never regret it, not for a second."

I brush my lips against his to give myself a few moments to make sense of all the words that I want to give August in response. I have a hundred different thoughts rushing through my brain and I need to try and focus on what I'm going to say. I take a deep breath and jump in with both feet. "Before tonight I never looked at you as anything other than my best friend. You are one of the most important people in my life but you were always just my brother."

I feel August tense against me so I rush to continue with what I need to say.

"Then you kissed me and everything I thought I knew went to hell. I didn't think something as simple as your lips would make me look at you in a completely different light. How could I have known you for so long but not seen *you*?" I laugh at myself, knowing that I probably sound insane. I've always scoffed when people spoke about insta-lust, but I refuse to see what's happening here as that, I mean I've known him nearly my whole life. "I don't know how I feel about you, but I do know that I want you to keep kissing me. Will this become something more? I don't know, but I want to find out. I don't want to rush this but I want to keep touching you, is that okay?" I don't know if he will understand what I'm trying to say so I just smile and hope he isn't about to kill a dream I didn't have until he touched me. I know he says that he's wanted me for years but that doesn't mean that he wants more. He might have wanted to live out a fantasy of kissing me and now he's done that he's about to walk away.

"I think I'm okay with that." His smile in this moment makes me want to stare at him forever. I've always thought August was attractive, I mean, who wouldn't? He's tall with jet-black hair that lies over his forehead and almost covers his eyes. His body is wide with muscles that could make a sane man crazy. He was always slightly small for his age but puberty made it up to him by giving him a body to die for. His eyes are dark and you can see every emotion in them when he looks at you, and tonight they are filled with an emotion that I've never seen before. I want to say it's love but I'm not going there, so I calm my racing heart by saying it's lust.

August bends his head and rests his forehead against mine. He takes a deep breath and when he exhales out I feel the heat all over my face. My eyes drift closed and a feeling of rightness comes over me as we just stand together. The way he's holding me with his hands gripping my hips like he doesn't want to let me go feels so intimate and surprisingly natural. It feels like we've done this all our lives.

For the first time since Ray's death I think it might be possible to fall in love again. I just never dreamed that it might be with my best friend.

CHAPTER FIVE

August

I lie and stare at the ceiling, loving the feel of Tristen lying in my bed close to me. This isn't how I imagined the night going when I had planned his birthday bash but I don't regret a moment of it. When I kissed Tristen I had assumed that he would come home and pack his bags. I never in my wildest dreams thought that he would kiss me back.

After confessing to him that I had always wanted to kiss him and listening to him say that he wanted to see where things would go, we had kissed for a while longer before moving to my bed. Now we are both lying together, a comfortable silence falling between the both of us. We will need to discuss this thing between us soon but I just want to live in our happy little bubble for a little while longer. Unfortunately Tristen doesn't feel the same way.

"We need to talk about this."

"I know, but it scares me." I might as well be completely honest with him from this point onwards. If me kissing him didn't send him running then there's a good chance that nothing will.

"Why?" Tristen turns until he's lying on his side, his head resting on his hand that's leaning on my chest.

"Because I don't want to lose you and admitting how I feel might do that. I've had a lot longer to get used to this than you, and I have a sneaking suspicion that my feelings are a little more intense than yours." I turn my head and look at him, hoping he can see the truth in my eyes. The love I have for Tristen runs deep and it will never change.

"Can you give me a little time to catch up with you?"

This man is fucking amazing. After everything he's been through over the last few years, here he is making sure that I feel comfortable. He should want to punch me for kissing him without permission, instead he's taking it all in his stride. "I would wait forever for you. I've already waited over half my life, what's another few years?"

He looks away from me quickly but not before I see colour heating his cheeks. "Why didn't you say anything?"

"To begin with it was because we were young. You instantly became the only friend I ever wanted and I didn't want to ruin that. Then I was confused about my sexuality and when I realised I was gay you hadn't come out yet. What straight guy wants his gay friend hitting on him?"

Tristen smiles and I think back to when we were younger. We were inseparable to the point where our parents even got into the habit of booking places for both of us when they were organising holidays. My parents once tried to go away without Tristen and I spent the whole two weeks moping and refusing to do anything with them so it never happened again.

"I didn't come out that long after you."

"No, but it was enough that I knew that I needed to let you go out and experience what you needed to. I didn't want to take that freedom from you. I remember what it was like to come out, to finally be comfortable in your own skin and I wanted you forever. Then you met Garry and I missed my chance. You were with him for so long that I honestly thought that you would marry him."

"So did I, until I saw him with his dick inside Dylan. It's amazing how seeing something like that quickly makes you see sense."

My anger grows when I think about how much Garry had hurt Tristen. He doesn't know but a month after they broke up, I saw Garry at a friend's party and let's just say that he left with a black eye and was walking funny. Tristen would be pissed if he knew I had given Garry a beating. He never wanted me to stand up for him in case I got into trouble. "I didn't want to be the arsehole that made a move on you when you had had your heart broken, and when you finally got over him enough to move on you found Ray. It felt like we weren't meant to be and I told myself that you and Ray would be together forever."

Tristen brings his eyes back up to look at me and I can see the sadness swimming in them. "I thought that too. If he hadn't have died, I think we would have been."

He looks embarrassed by his own honesty but I'm glad that he's being truthful with me. I know what he felt for Ray and truthfully it scares me a little. I'm worried that I will always feel like I'm trying to compete with a dead man, but it's something I'm willing to live with to be with Tristen. "You loved him so much and I was so happy for you ... I just couldn't be around it and watch."

"Is that why you stopped coming around?"

"Yeah, and I'm so sorry. I know it was a shitty thing to do but watching you together hurt too much." Tristen reaches out and brushes his fingers against my cheek and I close my eyes to allow myself to enjoy the feeling of him touching me.

"I wish you had told me at some point."

I open my eyes and look at him. "There was never a good time. That's why I asked you to tell me when you were ready to move on. I wanted to tell you but I didn't want to get the timing wrong." I feel the lump in my throat grow and I think about not saying the next words but I know I have to. My voice is thick with emotion as I speak. "I wanted to tell you that I was right here waiting for you."

Tristen moves quickly and before I know it, he's lying on top of my chest attacking my lips with his. This isn't a kiss of passion like the ones in the bathroom. This is something else, something more, something better. I know he doesn't love me, or at least not in the way that I want him to, but I don't care. At this moment in my life just having him here in my arms is enough.

I don't have a crystal ball so I don't know where all this might lead, or even if we will be together in six months, but every second I get to spend with Tristen like this will be my own personal heaven. He's all I ever imagined when I pictured my future. I wanted him by my side as I took on everything life threw at me. It was a simple dream but it was all I ever wanted. My parents didn't have a lot of spare money as I grew up. Enough to treat us to a holiday every few years, not abroad but we didn't care, we got to spend time together. What we missed out on in the latest fashions or the latest games, we got back in unconditional love. They loved me and my brother as much as humanly possible and they taught us that the true measurement of a life well spent was how much love it was filled with when we took our final breath.

Tristen stops kissing me but he doesn't move off of me. He lifts a hand and runs his fingers across my lips so I flick my tongue out and wet them. His eyes heat but he doesn't let me distract him from what he obviously wants to say. "I can't promise you forever, August. I wish I could but I don't want to lie to you. What I can promise is to give you everything that I'm able to. My heart was broken when Garry cheated on me, then again when Ray died and I didn't think I would survive, but I did. The only reason I did was because of *you*. You put me back together when there were too many broken pieces for me to do it by myself. You gave me back my life and I want to share it with you. This is all happening really fast, well maybe not for you, but it is for me, and I don't want to ruin it by rushing things. Let's go slow and enjoy this new journey."

I swear he's trying to make me cry. Everything he's saying makes so much sense and I smile under his fingertips. "Does that mean I have to buy you flowers and take you out to dinner?"

A smile tugs at the edge of Tristen's mouth but he recovers quickly. "Of course. I am not cheap Mr Reid, if you want me to put out then you are gonna have to treat me like a princess."

"So I need to buy you a tiara?" I've always loved our banter, the way we can tease each other without any offense being taken. I think that's what I would have hated the most if this hadn't turned out well, I would be losing the most important person in my life. I want to add to that relationship, develop it into something more, something special, but the most important thing will always be the friendship between us.

"Hell yeah you do. I don't want this to start on the wrong foot so let me give you a heads up. Diamonds are always a yes. Flowers are good but not lilies because my eyes will react. Take away as you know is a sure fire way to get you in my good books, because food is my favourite thing *ever*."

I lean up and kiss Tristen, biting his bottom lip slightly before lying back down. "You're a dork."

"You already knew this and yet you still kissed me, so who's the fool?"

"That would be me, but I would do it again and again."

He smiles and my heart melts at the sight. I saw him smiling like this with Garry and then with Ray, but I never dared let myself believe that I might be on the receiving end of it. It's the smile he gives when he's truly happy and when he feels that life is going well. It's the smile he's always given to the men he loves. "You need to go to bed."

Tristen looks confused and sits up. I follow him until were sitting facing each other. "Are you kicking me out of your room?"

"Yes, because if you don't leave now I won't be able to stick to your '*go slow*' plan. I can't have you here lying in my bed. It's a temptation I won't be able to resist. So go, now, for your own safety." I wink at him so he knows that even though I'm being deadly serious, there's no anger in what I'm saying.

"Fine. Can I have one last kiss before I go?"

It's testing the full limit of my control but I need to kiss him one last time before he leaves. I actually need to kiss him as much as possible for the rest of my life but I will start with this one. I lean in and give him a brief kiss but I try to fill it with every ounce of passion I'm feeling. "Go, now." My voice is slightly hoarse when I pull away. This is what he's always done to me. He leaves me breathless but this is the first night that it's been from kissing. Usually it's just watching him be the person he is. He makes everyone around him want to be a better person, even if it's just to get his attention.

I watch as Tristen gets up from my bed and heads towards the door. He gives me a little wave before he walks away, leaving me sitting and staring at the closed door like a crazy person. I take a minute to process everything that happened tonight because I don't want to forget a single moment of it. From feeling that I had lost him again to sharing my bed with him, this has been the most important night of my life.

A simple night out for Tristen's thirtieth birthday has changed my entire life and I couldn't be happier.

THE END

ABOUT THE AUTHOR

For more information on T.a. McKay

www.authortamckay.com
tamckayauthor@gmail.com

ALSO BY T.A. MCKAY

Leaving Marks series:

Leaving His Mark - Out now

Leaving Her Mark - Out now

Hard To Love series:

Worth The Fight - Out now

Make Me Trust - Out now

This Isn't Me - Out now

Standalone Novels:

Undercover - Out now

Someone To Hear Me - Out now

Coming soon:

Unsuspected

Asher

Satan's Crush

Printed in Poland
by Amazon Fulfillment
Poland Sp. z o.o., Wrocław